MW01155115

Extending Fractions
Grade 5

Table of Contents

Free Video Tutorial

 Use this QR code to launch a short video that provides instruction for skills featured in this book. To access the video from your smartphone or tablet:

- Download a free QR code scanner from your device's app store.
- Launch the scanning app on your device.
- Scan the code to visit the web page for this book.
- Find the video under the Resources tab.

This *Spectrum Focus* video is also available at:
- http://www.carsondellosa.com/704908
- www.youtube.com/user/CarsonDellosaPub

Spectrum®
An imprint of Carson-Dellosa Publishing LLC
P.O. Box 35665
Greensboro, NC 27425

ISBN 978-1-4838-2424-6

01-204157784

Focus On Extending Fractions

Understanding fractional numbers is a crucial part of the strong foundation needed for studying algebra and higher-level mathematics. As students gain skill and confidence in working with fractions, they are ready to add and subtract fractions with unlike denominators to solve equations and word problems. Fractions can be understood as the division of the numerator by the denominator. Multiplying fractions is used to scale measurements and to solve real-world problems. Finally, visual models and the relationship between multiplication and division can be used to divide unit fractions and whole numbers. For each of these skills, *Extending Fractions* provides step-by-step teaching, explanations, and practice.

Adding and Subtracting Fractions with Unlike Denominators

To add and subtract fractions with unlike denominators, first make the denominators the same. For both fractions in the equation, create equivalent fractions that share a common denominator. Use the lowest common multiple of the two denominators to create common denominators. Or, multiply the numerator and denominator of each fraction by the denominator of the other fraction in the equation as shown below.

$$\frac{3}{4} + \frac{4}{6} =$$

$$\frac{3 \times 6}{4 \times 6} = \frac{18}{24} \qquad \frac{4 \times 4}{6 \times 4} = \frac{16}{24}$$

$$\frac{4}{5} - \frac{1}{2} =$$

$$\frac{4 \times 2}{5 \times 2} = \frac{8}{10} \qquad \frac{1 \times 5}{2 \times 5} = \frac{5}{10}$$

Now that the denominators are the same, add or subtract the numerators. The denominator stays the same in the sum or difference. If possible, simplify.

$$\frac{18}{24} + \frac{16}{24} = \frac{34}{24} = 1\frac{10}{24} = 1\frac{5}{12}$$

$$\frac{8}{10} - \frac{5}{10} = \frac{3}{10}$$

Focus On Extending Fractions

Adding and Subtracting Mixed Numbers with Unlike Denominators

To add or subtract mixed numbers with unlike denominators, first add or subtract the whole numbers. Look at the example below.

$$1\frac{1}{2} + 2\frac{1}{3} = 3 + \frac{1}{2} + \frac{1}{3}$$

Next, change the two fractions in the equation into equivalent fractions with common denominators.

$$\frac{1 \times 3}{2 \times 3} = \frac{3}{6} \qquad\qquad \frac{1 \times 2}{3 \times 2} = \frac{2}{6}$$

Add or subtract the numerators. The denominator stays the same.

$$\frac{3}{6} + \frac{2}{6} = \frac{5}{6}$$

Finally, put the whole number and the fraction together for the complete answer: $3\frac{5}{6}$.

Solving Word Problems by Adding and Subtracting Fractions

Look at this word problem.

> Lorne and his brother Sheldon ate a pizza dinner. Lorne ate $\frac{3}{8}$ of the cheese pizza and $\frac{5}{12}$ of the vegetable pizza. Sheldon ate $\frac{1}{4}$ of the cheese pizza and $\frac{1}{2}$ of the vegetable pizza. How much was left of each pizza?

Before you begin to solve the problem, think about the fractions. Estimating will give you a good idea of what the solution should be. Think about the cheese pizza. One brother ate $\frac{3}{8}$ of it, which is close to $\frac{4}{8}$ or $\frac{1}{2}$ of the pizza. The other brother ate $\frac{1}{4}$ of the cheese pizza. You know that one half plus one quarter is three quarters, so about one quarter of the cheese pizza was uneaten. Making an estimate for how much of the vegetable pizza remained is similar. Lorne ate $\frac{5}{12}$ of it, which is close to $\frac{6}{12}$ or $\frac{1}{2}$. Sheldon ate $\frac{1}{2}$ of the vegetable pizza. You know that one half plus one half equals a whole, so only a small fraction of the vegetable pizza remained uneaten.

Now, write equations and solve the problem. First, find the total amount eaten from each pizza. Create equivalent fractions with common denominators before adding.

$\frac{3}{8} + \frac{1}{4}$ of the cheese pizza was eaten. $\frac{5}{12} + \frac{1}{2}$ of the vegetable pizza was eaten.

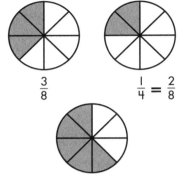   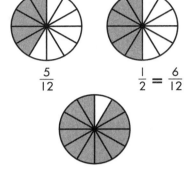

$\frac{3}{8}$ $\frac{1}{4} = \frac{2}{8}$ $\frac{5}{12}$ $\frac{1}{2} = \frac{6}{12}$

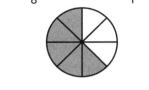

$\frac{5}{8}$ of the cheese pizza was eaten. $\frac{11}{12}$ of the vegetable pizza was eaten.

Finally, subtract the total eaten from each whole pizza. Represent whole numbers using the same denominator to make subtraction easy.

$\frac{8}{8} - \frac{5}{8} = \frac{3}{8}$ of the cheese pizza $\frac{12}{12} - \frac{11}{12} = \frac{1}{12}$ of the vegetable pizza
was left.   was left.

Now that you have solved the problem, think about the estimates you made. Was about one quarter of the cheese pizza left? (Yes, $\frac{3}{8}$ is close to $\frac{2}{8}$ or one quarter.) Was only a small fraction of the vegetable pizza left? (Yes, $\frac{1}{12}$ is a small fraction of the whole pizza.)

Dividing the Numerator by the Denominator

You know that fractions show parts of a whole. But, a fraction also shows division. The bar that separates the numerator from the denominator is called the *division bar*. It shows that the numerator is divided by the denominator. Look at these equivalent expressions.

$$\frac{3}{4} = \text{three divided by four} = 3 \div 4$$

The quotient of this division shows a portion of the whole. Three divided by 4 is 0.75. This decimal number is equivalent to the fraction $\frac{3}{4}$.

Focus On Extending Fractions

Solving Word Problems by Dividing Numerators by Denominators

Some word problems can be solved by creating a fraction that shows division. Look at this example.

> Each family made a different pasta dish for a family reunion. After the pasta feast, there were 5 equal-sized dishes of pasta left over. Joe wants to divide the leftover pasta into equal portions for 6 family members to take home. What fraction of the leftover pasta does each family member get?

You can draw a picture to show how Joe can divide the pasta.

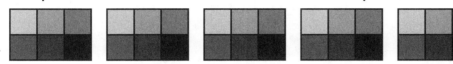

Since there are 5 dishes of pasta left over, the numerator of the fraction that each family member gets is 5. Since the leftovers will be divided among 6 family members, the denominator of the fraction is 6. Each family member will get $\frac{5}{6}$ of the remaining pasta. The fraction $\frac{5}{6}$ shows that the 5 dishes of pasta are divided into 6 parts: $5 \div 6 = \frac{5}{6}$.

Multiplying Fractions

When you multiply fractions, you are finding a fraction of a fraction. The product will be less than either of the factors. To multiply two fractions, multiply the numerators and then multiply the denominators. If possible, simplify the product.

$$\frac{3}{4} \times \frac{4}{5} = \frac{3 \times 4}{4 \times 5} = \frac{12}{20} = \frac{3}{5}$$

You know that the formula $l \times w$ can be used to find the area of a rectangle that has whole-number measurements for its sides. You can use the same formula to find the area of a rectangle with side measurements that are fractions. Remember that the product (or area) will not be larger than the factors (side lengths).

Focus On Extending Fractions

> Jordan is planting a garden that is $\frac{3}{4}$ of an acre long and $\frac{4}{5}$ of an acre wide. What is the area of her garden?

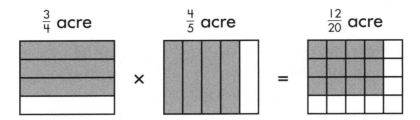

$\frac{3}{4}$ acre $\frac{4}{5}$ acre $\frac{12}{20}$ acre

To multiply mixed numbers, change each factor into an improper fraction. Then, multiply the numerators and denominators to find the product. Change the product into a fraction or mixed number in simplest form.

$$5\frac{2}{3} \times 3\frac{5}{8} = \frac{17}{3} \times \frac{29}{8} = \frac{493}{24} = 20\frac{13}{24}$$

Scaling (Resizing) by Multiplying Fractions

When you multiply a factor, you are making it larger or smaller. That is, you are *scaling* it up or down. If you are multiplying by a fraction, you can look at the factors and get an idea of what the scale of the product will be before you even start to solve the equation.

When you multiply a number by an improper fraction *greater* than 1, the product will be greater than the original number. When you multiply a number by a fraction *less* than 1, the product will be less than the original number.

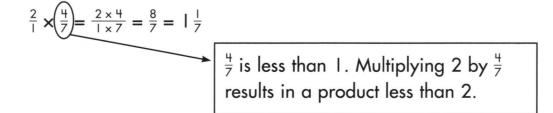

$$\frac{2}{1} \times \left(\frac{7}{4}\right) = \frac{2 \times 7}{1 \times 4} = \frac{14}{4} = 3\frac{2}{4} = 3\frac{1}{2}$$

$\frac{7}{4}$ is greater than 1. Multiplying 2 by $\frac{7}{4}$ results in a product greater than 2.

$$\frac{2}{1} \times \left(\frac{4}{7}\right) = \frac{2 \times 4}{1 \times 7} = \frac{8}{7} = 1\frac{1}{7}$$

$\frac{4}{7}$ is less than 1. Multiplying 2 by $\frac{4}{7}$ results in a product less than 2.

Focus On Extending Fractions

Here is another example of scaling.

$\frac{7}{8} \times \frac{5}{1}$ means you are increasing $\frac{7}{8}$ by 5 times.

$\frac{7}{8} =$ [bar model] $\qquad \frac{7}{8} \times \frac{5}{1} =$ [bar models] $\qquad = \frac{35}{8} = 4\frac{3}{8}$

$4\frac{3}{8} < 5$

Solving Word Problems by Multiplying Fractions

Many word problems can be solved by multiplying fractions. Study these examples.

> Marina bought 6 bags each containing $\frac{1}{2}$ pound of pistachios. How many pounds of pistachios did she buy altogether?

Think: Is the fraction greater than or less than 1? The fraction $\frac{1}{2}$ is less than 1, so the product will be less than 6.

Next, set up and solve the equation: $\frac{6}{1} \times \frac{1}{2}$. It may help to draw a model.

[six half-shaded bar models, each labeled $\frac{1}{2}$]

$$\frac{6}{1} \times \frac{1}{2} = \frac{6 \times 1}{1 \times 2} = \frac{6}{2} = 3$$

Marina bought 3 pounds of pistachios.

> Jared bought 1 slice of 8 different cheesecakes at a bake sale. Each cheesecake was the same size and was cut into 6 equal slices. How many whole cheesecakes did Jared buy?

Think: 1 slice of each cheesecake is $\frac{1}{6}$ of a cheesecake. There are 8 cheesecakes.

Next, set up and solve the equation $\frac{1}{6} \times \frac{8}{1} = \frac{1 \times 8}{6 \times 1} = \frac{8}{6} = 1\frac{2}{6} = 1\frac{1}{3}$.

Jared will buy a total of $1\frac{1}{3}$ cheesecakes. Because the number 8 was multiplied by a factor less than 1 ($\frac{1}{6}$), the product $1\frac{1}{3}$ is less than 8.

Dividing a Unit Fraction by a Whole Number

When you divide a unit fraction (a fraction with a numerator of 1) by a whole number, you are taking a fraction and dividing it into even smaller parts.

For example, if you have $\frac{1}{3}$ of a pie and want to divide that between 4 people, then that $\frac{1}{3}$ of the pie will get divided into 4 smaller parts. You could model this problem as follows.

 $\frac{1}{3} \div 4 = \frac{1}{12}$

Since multiplication and division are inverse operations, use multiplication to check your work.

$$\frac{1}{12} \times \frac{4}{1} = \frac{4}{12} = \frac{1}{3}$$

If $\frac{1}{3}$ of a pie is divided into 4 servings, each serving will be $\frac{1}{12}$ of the pie.

Dividing a Whole Number by a Unit Fraction

When you divide a whole number by a unit fraction (a fraction with a numerator of 1), you are increasing the number of wholes. For the equation $3 \div \frac{1}{4}$, you are dividing each of 3 wholes into 4.

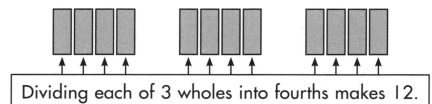
Dividing each of 3 wholes into fourths makes 12.

Use multiplication to check your work.

$$\frac{12}{1} \times \frac{1}{4} = \frac{12}{4} = \frac{3}{1} = 3$$

Focus On Extending Fractions

Solving Word Problems by Dividing

Many word problems can be solved by dividing. If you take time to picture what is being divided—the whole or the fraction—solving these problems will be easier. Study the examples.

> Ryan had $\frac{1}{5}$ a bag of chocolates. Ryan shared his chocolates with 3 friends. How much of the bag did each person get?

Think: What is being divided? One fifth of the bag of chocolates is being divided by 4 (Ryan + 3 friends). The fraction $\frac{1}{5}$ is being divided by 4.

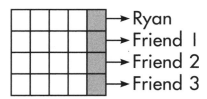

Ryan and his 3 friends will each get $\frac{1}{20}$ of the bag of chocolates. You know this is correct because $\frac{1}{20} \times \frac{4}{1} = \frac{4}{20} = \frac{1}{5}$.

> Sophia needs 3 cups of flour, but her only measuring cup is for $\frac{1}{3}$ cup. How many $\frac{1}{3}$-cup scoops will she need to measure 3 cups of flour?

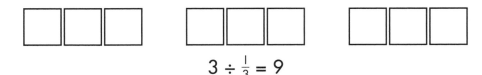

$$3 \div \frac{1}{3} = 9$$

Sophia will need 9 scoops (each measuring $\frac{1}{3}$ cup) to make her recipe. You know this is correct because $\frac{9}{1} \times \frac{1}{3} = \frac{9}{3} = \frac{3}{1} = 3$.

NAME _____

Guided Practice Unlike Denominators

Follow the directions. Write a number in each box.

1. Write multiples for each number. Circle the lowest common multiple.

6 ☐ ☐ ☐ ☐ ☐

15 ☐ ☐ ☐ ☐ ☐

2. Rewrite $\frac{3}{12}$ and $\frac{5}{8}$ using the least common multiple as a common denominator.

$$\frac{\Box}{\Box} \qquad \frac{\Box}{\Box}$$

3. Write equivalent fractions with common denominators. Add the numerators. The denominator stays the same.

$$\frac{2}{3} + \frac{1}{6}$$

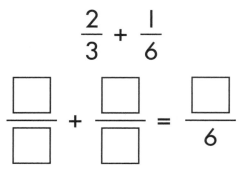

$$\frac{\Box}{\Box} + \frac{\Box}{\Box} = \frac{\Box}{6}$$

4. Write equivalent fractions with common denominators. Subtract the numerators. The denominator stays the same.

$$\frac{4}{5} - \frac{2}{7}$$

$$\frac{\Box}{\Box} - \frac{\Box}{\Box} = \frac{\Box}{\Box}$$

5. Rewrite the fractions with a common denominator and add. Combine the sum of the whole numbers and the sum of the fractions to find the sum.

$$4\frac{1}{6} + 2\frac{3}{4}$$

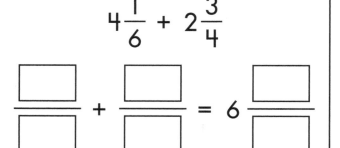

$$\frac{\Box}{\Box} + \frac{\Box}{\Box} = 6\frac{\Box}{\Box}$$

6. Rewrite the fractions with a common denominator and subtract. Combine the difference of the whole numbers and the difference of the fractions to find the difference.

$$9\frac{3}{6} - 7\frac{1}{3}$$

$$\frac{\Box}{\Box} - \frac{\Box}{\Box} = 2\frac{\Box}{\Box}$$

Independent Practice Unlike Denominators

Add or subtract. Write answers in simplest form.

1. $\dfrac{3}{8}$
$+\dfrac{1}{4}$

2. $\dfrac{2}{3}$
$+\dfrac{5}{9}$

3. $\dfrac{5}{12}$
$+\dfrac{7}{8}$

4. $\dfrac{1}{2}$
$+\dfrac{7}{10}$

5. $\dfrac{3}{4}$
$+\dfrac{5}{6}$

6. $\dfrac{5}{8}$
$-\dfrac{1}{9}$

7. $\dfrac{7}{10}$
$-\dfrac{7}{15}$

8. $\dfrac{8}{36}$
$-\dfrac{3}{14}$

9. $\dfrac{13}{36}$
$-\dfrac{9}{35}$

10. $\dfrac{10}{25}$
$-\dfrac{2}{9}$

11. $5\dfrac{7}{10}$
$+8\dfrac{2}{3}$

12. $11\dfrac{4}{5}$
$+\ 2\dfrac{8}{9}$

13. $6\dfrac{7}{8}$
$+5\dfrac{1}{6}$

14. $9\dfrac{5}{7}$
$+9\dfrac{9}{10}$

15. $5\dfrac{3}{4}$
$-4\dfrac{5}{8}$

16. $8\dfrac{2}{3}$
$-4\dfrac{1}{6}$

17. $5\dfrac{5}{6}$
$-3\dfrac{3}{4}$

18. $7\dfrac{4}{5}$
$-2\dfrac{1}{2}$

NAME _____

Guided Practice Dividing by the Denominator

Follow the directions. Write a number in each box.

1. Look at the improper fraction. Divide the numerator by the denominator. What is the quotient? $$\frac{42}{7} = \boxed{}$$	**2.** Look at the improper fraction. Divide the numerator by the denominator. What is the quotient? $$\frac{100}{10} = \boxed{}$$
3. Complete the division problem. $$\frac{2}{5} = 5\overline{)2.0}^{\,0.\boxed{}}$$	**4.** Complete the division problem. $$\frac{6}{10} = 10\overline{)6.0}^{\,0.\boxed{}}$$
5. Complete the second equation. $$\frac{1}{2} \times 2 = 1$$ $$1 \div 2 = \frac{\boxed{}}{\boxed{}}$$	**6.** Complete the second equation. $$\frac{3}{4} \times 4 = 3$$ $$3 \div 4 = \frac{\boxed{}}{\boxed{}}$$
7. Write a fraction to show that 9 easels are shared by 12 children. Simplify. 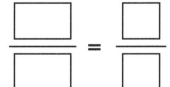	**8.** Write a fraction to show that 6 packages of paper are divided among 15 students. Simplify. 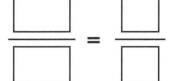

Independent Practice Dividing by the Denominator

Read each problem and answer the questions.

1. A 45-pound bag of rice is going to be split between 5 families. How much rice will each family receive?

   The way to write this as a division problem is _____ .

   The way to write this as a fraction is _____ .

   Each family will receive _____ pounds of rice.

2. A group of 3 students has to read a 21-page chapter for homework. How many pages will each student have to read if they are sharing the load?

   The way to write this as a division problem is _____ .

   The way to write this as a fraction is _____ .

   Each student will need to read _____ pages of the chapter.

Solve each problem. Give your answer as a fraction or mixed number in simplest form.

3. Chang has 16 cups of cake batter, and he plans to divide it evenly to make 24 cupcakes. How many cups of batter will be in each cupcake?

   _____ cup

4. Dominique needs 6 cups of dog food to feed her 4 dogs. If each dog gets the same amount of food, how many cups of food does each dog eat?

   _____ cups

5. Gabe needs to cut an 8-foot piece of plywood into 16 equivalent pieces for a fence. How wide will each piece be if all are the same length?

   _____ foot

6. A baker purchases flour in 25-pound bags and then separates it equally into 4 containers for storage. How many pounds of flour are in each container?

   _____ pounds

Guided Practice Multiplying Fractions

Follow the directions. Write a number in each box.

---

1. Look at the model. Write the product.

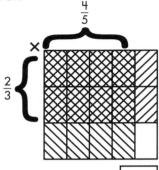

$$\frac{2}{3} \times \frac{4}{5} = \frac{\boxed{}}{15}$$

---

2. Look at the model. Write the product.

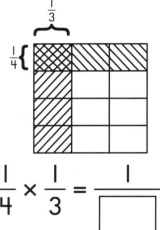

$$\frac{1}{4} \times \frac{1}{3} = \frac{1}{\boxed{}}$$

---

3. Multiply. Change the whole number into a fraction by writing it over a denominator of 1. Simplify the product.

$$\frac{8}{\boxed{}} \times \frac{2}{7} = \frac{16}{\boxed{}} = 2\frac{\boxed{}}{\boxed{}}$$

---

4. Multiply. Change the whole number into a fraction by writing it over a denominator of 1. Simplify the product.

$$\frac{3}{16} \times \frac{2}{\boxed{}} = \frac{6}{\boxed{}} = \frac{\boxed{}}{\boxed{}}$$

---

5. To find the product, multiply the numerators. Multiply the denominators. Simplify.

$$\frac{1}{6} \times \frac{8}{9} = \frac{\boxed{}}{\boxed{}} = \frac{\boxed{}}{\boxed{}}$$

---

6. Multiply $4\frac{1}{2} \times 1\frac{2}{3}$. Change each mixed number into an improper fraction. Give the product in simplest form.

$$\frac{9}{\boxed{}} \times \frac{\boxed{}}{3} = \frac{45}{\boxed{}} = 7\frac{\boxed{}}{\boxed{}}$$

Independent Practice Multiplying Fractions

Multiply. Give answers in simplest form.

1. $5 \times \frac{3}{10} =$ _____

2. $\frac{2}{3} \times 3 =$ _____

3. $9 \times \frac{7}{8} =$ _____

4. $\frac{6}{11} \times 7 =$ _____

5. $\frac{5}{6} \times \frac{3}{8} =$ _____

6. $\frac{5}{9} \times \frac{3}{7} =$ _____

7. $\frac{6}{11} \times \frac{1}{6} =$ _____

8. $\frac{3}{5} \times \frac{2}{3} =$ _____

9. $5\frac{3}{5} \times 2\frac{1}{4} =$ _____

10. $6\frac{1}{3} \times 1\frac{2}{5} =$ _____

11. $9\frac{1}{2} \times 2\frac{2}{7} =$ _____

12. $2\frac{6}{7} \times 5\frac{1}{7} =$ _____

Find the area of each rectangle in square units.

13.

$3\frac{1}{2}$ cm

4 cm

_____ square cm

14.

$2\frac{3}{4}$ in.

8 in.

_____ square in.

15.

$15\frac{1}{2}$ ft.

3 ft.

_____ square ft.

Guided Practice Multiplication as Scaling

Follow the directions. Write a number in each box.

---

1. Circle the model that shows $10 \times 1\frac{1}{2}$.

　　　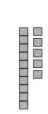

2. Circle the model that shows $10 \times \frac{1}{2}$.

　　　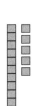

---

3. Complete the statement.

When a number is multiplied by a whole number greater than 1, by a mixed number, or by an improper fraction, the product will be _____ than the original number.

4. Complete the statement.

When a number is multiplied by a fraction or decimal number whose value is less than 1 whole, the product will be _____ than the original number.

---

5. Circle the larger number or expression.

$$100 \quad \text{or} \quad 100 \times 1\frac{3}{4}$$

6. Circle the larger number or expression.

$$4 \times \frac{7}{8} \quad \text{or} \quad 4$$

---

7. A slide for young children is 6 feet tall. A park director wants to order a slide for older children that is $1\frac{2}{3}$ times as tall. How tall should the new slide be? Solve the equation.

$$\frac{6}{1} \times \frac{5}{3} = \frac{\boxed{}}{\boxed{}} = \boxed{}$$

feet tall

8. A sailboat is 18 feet long. Thomas is building a model that is $\frac{1}{16}$ its size. How long will Thomas's model be?

$$\frac{18}{\boxed{}} \times \frac{\boxed{}}{\boxed{}} = \frac{18}{\boxed{}} = 1\frac{\boxed{}}{\boxed{}}$$

feet long

NAME _____

Independent Practice Multiplication as Scaling

Circle the number or expression that is greater.

1. 72 or $72 \times \frac{1}{3}$

2. $2\frac{1}{8} \times 24$ or 24

3. 1 or $1 \times \frac{15}{16}$

4. $\frac{2}{5} \times 225$ or $\frac{4}{5} \times 225$

5. 12×12 or $12 \times 5\frac{2}{3}$

6. 15×10 or 15×1

7. $\frac{1}{2} \times \frac{7}{8}$ or $\frac{1}{2} \times 5\frac{7}{8}$

8. $\frac{3}{5} \times 75$ or 75×1

9. $150 \times \frac{10}{12}$ or $150 \times \frac{1}{2}$

Circle the number or expression that is less.

10. $12 \times 5\frac{7}{8}$ or $12 \times \frac{7}{8}$

11. 52 or $52 \times 7\frac{1}{3}$

12. $50 \times \frac{1}{3}$ or $50 \times \frac{2}{3}$

13. $\frac{11}{12} \times 1$ or $1 \times \frac{12}{12}$

14. $\frac{2}{5} \times 8$ or 8

15. $50 \times \frac{7}{10}$ or 7×50

16. $19 \times \frac{3}{4}$ or $19 \times 3\frac{1}{4}$

17. 1×0.5 or 1×0.25

18. 20 or $20 \times \frac{5}{6}$

Solve.

19. At a kennel, a small dog's pen is 10 feet long and 8 feet wide. The area of a medium-sized dog's pen is $1\frac{3}{4}$ times as large. What is the area of a pen for a medium-sized dog?

The area is _____ square feet.

20. A flashlight with a strong battery can shine 4 meters ahead. A flashlight with a weak battery can shine $\frac{2}{5}$ that distance. How many meters ahead can the flashlight with the weak battery shine?

It can shine _____ meters ahead.

Spectrum Focus: Extending Fractions
Grade 5

Independent Practice

17

NAME _____

Guided Practice Dividing Unit Fractions

Follow the directions. Write a number in each box.

1. Draw lines on the model to show $\frac{1}{4} \div 4 = \frac{1}{16}$. Divide each fourth into fourths.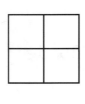

2. Draw lines on the model to show $\frac{1}{6} \div 2 = \frac{1}{12}$. Divide each sixth into halves.

3. Use the model to help you find the quotient.

$$\frac{1}{5} \div 3 = \frac{\boxed{}}{\boxed{}}$$

4. Look at the model. Complete the equation.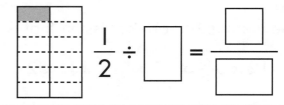

$$\frac{1}{2} \div \boxed{} = \frac{\boxed{}}{\boxed{}}$$

5. Solve the equation. Draw a model to help you.

$$\frac{1}{6} \div 6 = \frac{\boxed{}}{\boxed{}}$$

6. Solve the equation. Draw a model to help you.

$$\frac{1}{8} \div 3 = \frac{\boxed{}}{\boxed{}}$$

7. Use the multiplication equation to help you find the quotient.

$$4 \times \frac{1}{48} = \frac{1}{12}$$

$$\frac{1}{12} \div 4 = \frac{\boxed{}}{\boxed{}}$$

8. Use the multiplication equation to help you find the quotient.

$$\frac{1}{40} \times 5 = \frac{1}{8}$$

$$\frac{1}{8} \div 5 = \frac{\boxed{}}{\boxed{}}$$

Independent Practice Dividing Unit Fractions

Write each quotient. Draw a model to help you.

1. $\frac{1}{4} \div 7 =$

2. $\frac{1}{3} \div 3 =$

3. $\frac{1}{5} \div 9 =$

4. $\frac{1}{2} \div 6 =$

5. $\frac{1}{2} \div 7 =$

6. $\frac{1}{6} \div 2 =$

7. $\frac{1}{8} \div 3 =$

8. $\frac{1}{7} \div 2 =$

9. Three cousins will split $\frac{1}{4}$ of a cherry pie. What fraction of the pie will each cousin get? Solve the multiplication equation. Then, write a division equation to solve the word problem.

Multiplication equation: Division equation:

$3 \times \frac{1}{12} =$ _____

_____ of the pie

10. Ms. Garcia has $\frac{1}{2}$ pound of birdseed. What fraction of a pound can she put in a bird feeder for each of 5 days? Solve the multiplication equation. Then, write a division equation to solve the word problem.

Multiplication equation: Division equation:

$5 \times \frac{1}{10} =$ _____

_____ of the birdseed

Guided Practice Dividing Whole Numbers

Follow the directions. Write a number in each box.

1. Draw lines on the model to show $4 \div \frac{1}{5} = 20$. Show that each whole gets divided into 5.

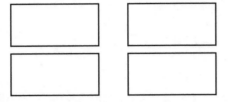

2. Draw lines on the model to show $8 \div \frac{1}{6} = 48$. Show that each whole gets divided into 6.

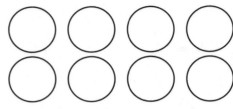

3. Use the model to help you find the quotient.

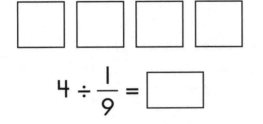

$$4 \div \frac{1}{9} = \boxed{}$$

4. Look at the model. Complete the equation.

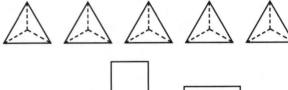

$$5 \div \frac{\boxed{}}{\boxed{}} = \boxed{}$$

5. Solve the equation. Draw a model to help you.

$$6 \div \frac{1}{4} = \boxed{}$$

6. Solve the equation. Draw a model to help you.

$$9 \div \frac{1}{6} = \boxed{}$$

7. Use the multiplication equation to help you find the quotient.

$$14 \times \frac{1}{2} = 7$$

$$7 \div \frac{1}{2} = \boxed{}$$

8. Use the multiplication equation to help you find the quotient.

$$90 \times \frac{1}{10} = 9$$

$$9 \div \frac{1}{10} = \boxed{}$$

Independent Practice Dividing Whole Numbers

Write each quotient. Draw a model to help you.

1. $5 \div \dfrac{1}{7} =$

2. $3 \div \dfrac{1}{9} =$

3. $15 \div \dfrac{1}{8} =$

4. $6 \div \dfrac{1}{7} =$

5. $11 \div \dfrac{1}{2} =$

6. $19 \div \dfrac{1}{3} =$

7. $8 \div \dfrac{1}{9} =$

8. $18 \div \dfrac{1}{5} =$

9. Victor has 7 yards of string. He needs $\frac{1}{3}$ yard of string for each of the puppets he is making. How many puppets can Victor make with his string? Solve the multiplication equation. Then, write a division equation to solve the word problem.

Multiplication equation:

Division equation:

$\dfrac{1}{3} \times \dfrac{21}{1} = \underline{\hspace{1cm}}$

$\underline{\hspace{4cm}}$ puppets

10. Phoebe and her dad cleaned the basement for 4 hours on Saturday. They took a break every $\frac{1}{2}$ hour. How many breaks did they take? Solve the multiplication equation. Then, write a division equation to solve the word problem.

Multiplication equation:

Division equation:

$\dfrac{1}{2} \times \dfrac{8}{1} = \underline{\hspace{1cm}}$

$\underline{\hspace{4cm}}$ breaks

NAME _____

Guided Practice Word Problems

Write a number in each box to set up equations and solve the word problems.

1. The Rizzo's farm has $9\frac{1}{2}$ acres of corn and $7\frac{1}{3}$ acres of soybeans. How many acres altogether are planted at the Rizzo farm?

$$9\frac{1}{2} + 7\frac{1}{3} = 9\frac{\Box}{6} + 7\frac{\Box}{\Box} = 16\frac{\Box}{\Box} \text{ acres}$$

2. Aimee lives $\frac{8}{9}$ mile from the park. She has walked $\frac{3}{5}$ of the way. How far has Aimee walked?

$$\frac{\Box}{\Box} \times \frac{\Box}{\Box} = \frac{\Box}{45} = \frac{\Box}{\Box} \text{ mile}$$

3. A single smoothie requires $\frac{1}{8}$ cup orange juice. How much orange juice is needed for 6 smoothies?

$$\frac{6}{\Box} \times \frac{\Box}{\Box} = \frac{\Box}{\Box} = \frac{\Box}{\Box} \text{ cup orange juice}$$

4. A $\frac{1}{2}$-hour television show is divided into 3 parts between commercial breaks. How long is each part? Complete the multiplication equation. Then, complete the division equation to solve the problem.

$$\frac{3}{1} \times \frac{1}{6} = \frac{\Box}{\Box} = \frac{\Box}{\Box} \qquad \frac{1}{2} \div 3 = \frac{\Box}{\Box} \text{ of an hour}$$

NAME _____

Independent Practice Word Problems

Add, subtract, multiply, or divide to solve each word problem. Give answers in simplest form.

1. A fully inflated soccer ball weighs 6 ounces. Brian's ball is inflated to $4\frac{2}{3}$ ounces. How many more ounces of air are needed to fully inflate the ball?

   _____ ounces

2. Cara's gas tank has $5\frac{3}{5}$ gallons of gas in it. She adds $7\frac{2}{3}$ gallons. How many gallons of gas are in the tank now?

   _____ gallons

3. Simon has $\frac{3}{4}$ memory remaining on a 24-gigabyte memory card. How much memory does he have left?

   _____ gigabytes

4. Some toy cars are $2\frac{4}{5}$ inches long. How long are 6 of the cars laid end to end?

   _____ inches

5. Alexis bought $\frac{2}{3}$ pound of bananas and ate $\frac{4}{5}$ of what she bought. What was the weight of the bananas Alexis ate?

   _____ pound

6. One batch of pancakes calls for $1\frac{1}{3}$ cups of milk. How many cups of milk are needed for 4 batches?

   _____ cups

7. One third of an hour is spent listening to 6 songs. Each song lasts for what fraction of an hour? Use $\frac{6}{1} \times \frac{1}{18} = \frac{1}{3}$ to help you solve the problem.

   _____ hour

8. How many $\frac{1}{4}$-cup servings are in 2 cups of rice? Use $\frac{1}{4} \times \frac{8}{1} = 2$ to help you solve the problem.

   _____ servings

NAME _____

Performance Task 1

Solve

Solve the real-world problem. Use the space to show your mathematical thinking.

Mr. Taylor asked his grandsons to mow his yard. Jermaine mowed $\frac{1}{3}$ of the yard on Monday morning. Javon mowed part of the yard on Monday afternoon. Javon wanted to mow at least $\frac{1}{4}$ of the yard. Together, the grandsons mowed $\frac{17}{24}$ of the yard. Did Javon meet his goal?

Reflect

Explain the steps you used to form the equivalent fractions needed to solve the task.

_____

_____

_____

_____

_____

Performance Task 2

Solve

Solve the real-world problem. Use the space to show your mathematical thinking.

Mrs. Walter took her 3 children and 3 of their friends to a strawberry field. Mrs. Walter wanted each child to get at least $\frac{1}{4}$ pound of strawberries. They picked 2 pounds altogether. Did each child get the $\frac{1}{4}$ pound that Mrs. Walter wanted?

Reflect

Explain the steps you used to solve the task.

_____

_____

_____

_____

_____

_____

_____

Performance Task 3

Solve

Solve the real-world problem. Use the space to show your mathematical thinking.

Sam and Charlotte have been given areas in the community garden. Sam's garden area is $1\frac{1}{3}$ of 60 square feet. Charlotte's area is $\frac{9}{10}$ of Sam's area. They would like to plant corn. Because it is such a large crop, they need 150 square feet in all for the corn. Together, do Sam and Charlotte have enough area to plant the corn?

Reflect

What information helped you predict that Sam's area would be larger than 60 square feet?

_____

_____

_____

_____

_____

_____

Performance Task 4

Solve

Solve the real-world problem. Use the space to show your mathematical thinking.

Chang is making sand ornaments. His recipe requires $\frac{2}{3}$ cup of sand and makes 24 ornaments. He only wants to make 12 ornaments and has $\frac{3}{8}$ cup of sand. Does he have enough sand?

Reflect

Chang notices that when he multiplies fractions, his answer is always smaller than either original number. Is his observation correct? Explain.

_____

_____

_____

_____

_____

_____

Performance Task 5

Solve

Solve the real-world problem. Use the space to show your mathematical thinking.

Mr. Davis handed $\frac{1}{4}$ of a package of paper out to 6 students. The original package had 120 sheets in it. What fraction of the paper did each student get? Each student needs 4 sheets of paper to complete an assignment. Do they have enough paper? Draw a model to help solve the problem.

Reflect

What if the paper had to be divided among 8 students? Explain.

_____

_____

_____

_____

_____

_____

Assessment

Part 1: I can add and subtract fractions and mixed numbers with unlike denominators.

Rename each pair of fractions with common denominators.

1. $\dfrac{5}{12}$ and $\dfrac{4}{5}$ _____

2. $\dfrac{3}{8}$ and $\dfrac{5}{6}$ _____

3. $\dfrac{5}{9}$ and $\dfrac{1}{2}$ _____

Add or subtract. Write answers in simplest form.

4. $\dfrac{2}{9} + \dfrac{5}{8}$

5. $\dfrac{6}{7} + \dfrac{1}{3}$

6. $\dfrac{2}{5} + \dfrac{5}{7}$

7. $\dfrac{7}{10} + \dfrac{1}{3}$

8. $\dfrac{7}{10} - \dfrac{3}{6}$

9. $\dfrac{8}{9} - \dfrac{1}{4}$

10. $\dfrac{7}{8} - \dfrac{5}{12}$

11. $\dfrac{7}{10} - \dfrac{1}{4}$

12. $4\dfrac{2}{7} + 3\dfrac{3}{4}$

13. $5\dfrac{1}{4} + 2\dfrac{1}{5}$

14. $6\dfrac{6}{7} - 3\dfrac{3}{5}$

15. $5\dfrac{5}{6} - 3\dfrac{1}{12}$

Assessment

Solve.

16. Mr. Ito cuts off $\frac{2}{5}$ meter from a rope that is 6 meters long. How much of the rope is left?

_____ meters

17. Tasha spent $\frac{1}{3}$ hour cleaning her room. Tyrone spent $\frac{3}{5}$ hour cleaning his room. Altogether, how long did the two spend cleaning their rooms?

_____ hour

Part 2: I can interpret a fraction as the division of the numerator by the denominator.

Write each fraction as a division problem.

1. $\frac{7}{12}$ _____

2. $\frac{8}{3}$ _____

3. $\frac{4}{5}$ _____

Write a fraction to express each situation.

4. 1 pound of clay used to make 5 bowls _____

5. 12 balls shared by 3 baseball teams _____

6. 50 reserved seats in a 150-seat theater _____

Part 3: I can multiply whole numbers and fractions by fractions.

Multiply. Write answers in simplest form.

1. $\frac{1}{4} \times \frac{8}{9} =$ ____

2. $\frac{3}{5} \times \frac{5}{6} =$ ____

3. $\frac{5}{7} \times \frac{1}{2} =$ ____

4. $\frac{11}{12} \times \frac{2}{3} =$ ____

5. $\frac{3}{7} \times \frac{4}{5} =$ ____

6. $\frac{3}{4} \times \frac{3}{8} =$ ____

7. $3 \times \frac{5}{8} =$ ____

8. $\frac{1}{6} \times 4 =$ ____

9. $\frac{1}{3} \times 9 =$ ____

Assessment

10. $2\frac{7}{8} \times 2 = $ _____

11. $1\frac{7}{12} \times 9 = $ _____

12. $3\frac{3}{10} \times 8 = $ _____

13. $\frac{1}{2} \times \frac{1}{3} = $ _____

14. $\frac{3}{4} \times \frac{2}{7} = $ _____

15. $\frac{1}{4} \times \frac{4}{5} = $ _____

16. $\frac{2}{5} \times \frac{5}{8} = $ _____

17. $\frac{4}{9} \times \frac{1}{2} = $ _____

18. $5 \times \frac{2}{7} = $ _____

Solve.

19.

$3\frac{4}{9}$ meters

$1\frac{2}{3}$ meters

Area = _____ square meters

20.

$26\frac{1}{2}$ miles

$17\frac{7}{8}$ miles

Area = _____ square miles

21. Boxes of winter clothes weigh $10\frac{1}{2}$ pounds each. How much do 4 of the boxes weigh?

_____ pounds

22. Only $\frac{2}{3}$ of students took their permission slips home. Only $\frac{1}{8}$ of those students got the slips signed. What fraction of all the students got their permission slips signed?

_____ of the students

Part 4: I can interpret multiplication as scaling.

Circle the number or expression that is greater.

1. 1 or $1 \times \frac{1}{2}$

2. $9 \times \frac{5}{8}$ or $9 \times \frac{7}{8}$

3. $1{,}000 \times 2\frac{2}{3}$ or $1{,}000 \times \frac{1}{3}$

4. $100 \times \frac{1}{10}$ or 100×10

5. $82 \times 1\frac{1}{16}$ or 82

6. 698×0.75 or 698

Assessment

Solve.

7. A new building will be 38 feet tall. A model of the building is $\frac{1}{8}$ that height. How tall is the model?

_____ feet tall

8. A recipe calls for 3 cups of strawberries. To make $2\frac{3}{4}$ batches of the recipe, how many cups of strawberries would be needed?

_____ cups

Part 5: I can use models and the relationship between multiplication and division to divide unit fractions by whole numbers and whole numbers by unit fractions.

Write each quotient. Draw a model to help you.

1. $\frac{1}{4} \div 12 =$ _____

2. $\frac{1}{8} \div 6 =$ _____

3. $\frac{1}{7} \div 2 =$ _____

4. $5 \div \frac{1}{9} =$ _____

5. $10 \div \frac{1}{6} =$ _____

6. $6 \div \frac{1}{9} =$ _____

Solve each multiplication equation. Then, write a related division equation.

7. $5 \times \frac{1}{90} =$ _____

Division equation: _____

8. $36 \times \frac{1}{9} =$ _____

Division equation: _____

Answer Key

Page 10

1. 6, 12, 18, 24, (30) and 15, (30) 45, 60, 75;
2. $\frac{6}{24}$, $\frac{15}{24}$; 3. $\frac{4}{6} + \frac{1}{6} = \frac{5}{6}$; 4. $\frac{28}{35} - \frac{10}{35} = \frac{18}{35}$;
5. $4\frac{2}{12} + 2\frac{9}{12} = 6\frac{11}{12}$; 6. $9\frac{3}{6} - 7\frac{2}{6} = 2\frac{1}{6}$

Page 11

1. $\frac{5}{8}$; 2. $1\frac{2}{9}$; 3. $1\frac{7}{24}$; 4. $1\frac{1}{5}$; 5. $1\frac{7}{12}$; 6. $\frac{37}{72}$;
7. $\frac{7}{30}$; 8. $\frac{1}{126}$; 9. $\frac{131}{260}$; 10. $\frac{8}{45}$; 11. $14\frac{11}{30}$;
12. $14\frac{31}{45}$; 13. $12\frac{1}{24}$; 14. $19\frac{43}{70}$; 15. $1\frac{1}{8}$;
16. $4\frac{1}{2}$; 17. $2\frac{1}{12}$; 18. $5\frac{3}{10}$

Page 12

1. 6; 2. 10; 3. 0.4; 4. 0.6; 5. $1 \div 2 = \frac{1}{2}$;
6. $3 \div 4 = \frac{3}{4}$; 7. $\frac{9}{12} = \frac{3}{4}$; 8. $\frac{6}{15} = \frac{2}{5}$

Page 13

1. $45 \div 5$, $\frac{45}{5}$, 9; 2. $21 \div 3$, $\frac{21}{3}$, 7;
3. $\frac{16}{24} = \frac{2}{3}$ cup; 4. $\frac{6}{4} = 1\frac{1}{2}$ cups; 5. $\frac{8}{16} = \frac{1}{2}$ foot;
6. $\frac{25}{4} = 6\frac{1}{4}$ pounds

Page 14

1. $\frac{2}{3} \times \frac{4}{5} = \frac{8}{15}$; 2. $\frac{1}{4} \times \frac{1}{3} = \frac{1}{12}$; 3. $\frac{8}{1} \times \frac{2}{7} = \frac{16}{7} =$
$2\frac{2}{7}$; 4. $\frac{3}{16} \times \frac{2}{1} = \frac{6}{16} = \frac{3}{8}$; 5. $\frac{1}{6} \times \frac{8}{9} = \frac{8}{54} = \frac{4}{27}$;
6. $\frac{9}{2} \times \frac{5}{3} = \frac{45}{6} = 7\frac{1}{2}$

Page 15

1. $1\frac{1}{2}$; 2. 2; 3. $7\frac{7}{8}$; 4. $3\frac{9}{11}$; 5. $\frac{5}{16}$; 6. $\frac{5}{21}$;
7. $\frac{1}{11}$; 8. $\frac{2}{5}$; 9. $12\frac{3}{5}$; 10. $8\frac{13}{15}$; 11. $21\frac{5}{7}$;
12. $14\frac{34}{49}$; 13. 14 square cm; 14. 22 square
in.; 15. $46\frac{1}{2}$ square ft.

Page 16

1. ; 2. ; 3. greater; 4. less;
5. $100 \times 1\frac{3}{4}$; 6. 4; 7. $\frac{6}{1} \times \frac{5}{3} = \frac{30}{3} = 10$;
8. $\frac{18}{1} \times \frac{1}{16} = \frac{18}{16} = 1\frac{2}{16} = 1\frac{1}{8}$

Page 17

1. 72; 2. $2\frac{1}{8} \times 24$; 3. 1; 4. $\frac{4}{5} \times 225$;
5. 12×12; 6. 15×10; 7. $\frac{1}{2} \times 5\frac{7}{8}$;
8. 75×1; 9. $150 \times \frac{10}{12}$; 10. $12 \times \frac{7}{8}$; 11. 52;
12. $50 \times \frac{1}{3}$; 13. $\frac{11}{12} \times 1$; 14. $\frac{2}{5} \times 8$;
15. $50 \times \frac{7}{10}$; 16. $19 \times \frac{3}{4}$; 17. 1×0.25;
18. $20 \times \frac{5}{6}$; 19. 140; 20. $1\frac{3}{5}$

Page 18

1. ; 2. ; 3. , $\frac{1}{5} \div 3 = \frac{1}{15}$;
4. $\frac{1}{2} \div 6 = \frac{1}{12}$; 5. Students' drawings should
show 36 equal parts. $\frac{1}{6} \div 6 = \frac{1}{36}$; 6. Students'
drawings should show 24 equal parts.
$\frac{1}{8} \div 3 = \frac{1}{24}$; 7. $\frac{1}{12} \div 4 = \frac{1}{48}$; 8. $\frac{1}{8} \div 5 = \frac{1}{40}$

Page 19

1. $\frac{1}{28}$; 2. $\frac{1}{9}$; 3. $\frac{1}{45}$; 4. $\frac{1}{12}$; 5. $\frac{1}{14}$; 6. $\frac{1}{12}$; 7. $\frac{1}{24}$;
8. $\frac{1}{14}$; 9. $\frac{1}{4}$, $\frac{1}{4} \div 3 = \frac{1}{12}$ of the pie;
10. $\frac{1}{2}$, $\frac{1}{2} \div 5 = \frac{1}{10}$ of the birdseed

Answer Key

Page 20

1. ; 2. ;

3. , $4 \div \frac{1}{9} = 36$;

4. $5 \div \frac{1}{3} = 15$; 5. Students' drawings should show 6 shapes divided into fourths. $6 \div \frac{1}{4} = 24$; 6. Students' drawings should show 9 shapes divided into sixths. $9 \div \frac{1}{6} = 54$;

7. $7 \div \frac{1}{2} = 14$; 8. $9 \div \frac{1}{10} = 90$

Page 21

1. 35; 2. 27; 3. 120; 4. 42; 5. 22; 6. 57;
7. 72; 8. 90; 9. 7, $7 \div \frac{1}{3} = 21$ puppets;
10. 4, $4 \div \frac{1}{2} = 8$ breaks

Page 22

1. $9\frac{3}{6} + 7\frac{2}{6} = 16\frac{5}{6}$; 2. $\frac{8}{9} \times \frac{3}{5} = \frac{24}{45} = \frac{8}{15}$;
3. $\frac{6}{1} \times \frac{1}{8} = \frac{6}{8} = \frac{3}{4}$; 4. $\frac{3}{1} \times \frac{1}{6} = \frac{3}{6} = \frac{1}{2}$, $\frac{1}{2} \div 3 = \frac{1}{6}$

Page 23

1. $1\frac{1}{3}$; 2. $13\frac{4}{15}$; 3. 18; 4. $16\frac{4}{5}$; 5. $\frac{8}{15}$; 6. $5\frac{1}{3}$;
7. $\frac{1}{18}$; 8. 8

Page 24

Solve: Proficient students will subtract $\frac{1}{3}$ (the amount of the yard that Jermaine mowed) from $\frac{17}{24}$ (the total amount of the yard that was mowed) by rewriting the fractions with common denominators so that the problem becomes $\frac{17}{24} - \frac{8}{24} = \frac{9}{24} = \frac{3}{8}$. So, the part of the yard that was mowed by Javon was $\frac{3}{8}$. Javon wanted to mow at least $\frac{1}{4}$ of the yard. To compare the fractions $\frac{3}{8}$ and $\frac{1}{4}$, students should rewrite them with common denominators as $\frac{3}{8}$ and $\frac{2}{8}$ to discover that, since $\frac{3}{8}$ is more than $\frac{2}{8}$ (or $\frac{1}{4}$), Javon did mow at least $\frac{1}{4}$ of the yard.

Reflect: To rewrite the fractions $\frac{1}{3}$ and $\frac{17}{24}$ with common denominators, find multiples of 3 (3, 6, 12, 24…) and multiples of 24 (24, 48, 72…). The lowest common multiple in the two lists is 24, so use 24 as a common denominator. To rewrite $\frac{1}{3}$ as an equivalent fraction with the denominator 24, multiply 3 (the denominator) by 8 and 1 (the numerator) by 8 to get the equivalent fraction $\frac{8}{24}$.

Page 25

Solve: Proficient students will observe that the solution can be expressed as the fraction $\frac{2}{6}$ which shows the division problem 2 (pounds of strawberries picked) divided by 6 (number of children). The fraction $\frac{2}{6}$ can be simplified to $\frac{1}{3}$, so each child picked $\frac{1}{3}$ pound of strawberries. Since $\frac{1}{3}$ is greater than $\frac{1}{4}$, Mrs. Walter's goal of having each child pick at least $\frac{1}{4}$ pound of strawberries was met.

Answer Key

Reflect: In order to solve the problem, find the dividend 2 (for 2 pounds of strawberries) and divide it by the divisor 6 (number of children picking strawberries). This division problem can be expressed as a fraction.

Page 26

Solve: Proficient students will calculate the area of Sam's garden as 60 (square feet) × $1\frac{1}{3}$ = 80 square feet. The area of Charlotte's garden can be calculated as 80 (square feet of Sam's garden) × $\frac{9}{10}$ = 72 square feet. Since 80 + 72 = 152 square feet, Sam and Charlotte do have enough space to plant corn, which requires at least 150 square feet of garden space.

Reflect: Since the area of Sam's garden can be calculated by multiplying 60 by a factor greater than 1 ($1\frac{1}{3}$), you know that the total area will be more than 60 square feet.

Page 27

Solve: Proficient students will find the amount of sand that Chang needs to make 12 ornaments by multiplying $\frac{2}{3}$ (cups of sand needed to make 24 ornaments) by $\frac{1}{2}$ (since Chang wants to make only $\frac{1}{2}$ of the recipe) to get a product of $\frac{2}{6}$ or $\frac{1}{3}$. Chang has $\frac{3}{8}$ cup of sand. To find out whether he has enough sand, compare $\frac{3}{8}$ (the amount of sand he has) to $\frac{1}{3}$ (the amount of sand needed) by rewriting the fractions with common denominators as $\frac{9}{24}$ and $\frac{8}{24}$. Since $\frac{9}{24}$ (or $\frac{3}{8}$) is larger than $\frac{8}{24}$ (or $\frac{1}{3}$), Chang does have enough sand to make 12 ornaments.

Reflect: Chang's observation is correct because when multiplying fractions, a factor less than 1 is multiplied by another factor less than 1. So, the product will always be smaller than either of the factors.

Page 28

Solve: Proficient students will draw a rectangle to represent the original package of paper and divide it into fourths. To divide $\frac{1}{4}$ by 6, they will divide each fourth of the rectangle into sixths to find that the package of paper is divided into 24 equal parts. This can be expressed $\frac{1}{4} \div 6 = \frac{1}{24}$. To find out how many sheets of paper are in $\frac{1}{24}$, students should calculate 120 (the number of sheets in the whole package of paper) × $\frac{1}{24}$ = 5. So, each of the 6 students will receive 5 sheets of paper. Since 5 is more than the 4 sheets of paper each student needs for the assignment, the students do have enough paper.

Reflect: If $\frac{1}{4}$ package of paper had to be divided among 8 students, each student would receive $\frac{1}{32}$ of the package since $\frac{1}{4} \div 8 = \frac{1}{32}$. Multiplying 120 × $\frac{1}{32}$ tells you that each student would receive only $3\frac{3}{4}$ sheets of paper, meaning that they wouldn't have enough paper for the assignment.

Answer Key

Assessment

Part 1: **1.** $\frac{25}{60}$, $\frac{48}{60}$; **2.** $\frac{9}{24}$, $\frac{20}{24}$; **3.** $\frac{10}{18}$, $\frac{9}{18}$;
4. $\frac{61}{72}$; **5.** $1\frac{4}{21}$; **6.** $1\frac{4}{35}$; **7.** $1\frac{1}{30}$; **8.** $\frac{1}{5}$; **9.** $\frac{23}{26}$;
10. $\frac{11}{24}$; **11.** $\frac{9}{20}$; **12.** $8\frac{1}{28}$; **13.** $7\frac{9}{20}$; **14.** $3\frac{9}{35}$;
15. $2\frac{3}{4}$; **16.** $5\frac{3}{5}$; **17.** $\frac{14}{15}$

Part 2: **1.** $7 \div 12$; **2.** $8 \div 3$; **3.** $4 \div 5$; **4.** $\frac{1}{5}$;
5. $\frac{12}{3}$; **6.** $\frac{50}{150}$

Part 3: **1.** $\frac{2}{9}$; **2.** $\frac{1}{2}$; **3.** $\frac{5}{14}$; **4.** $\frac{11}{18}$; **5.** $\frac{12}{35}$; **6.** $\frac{9}{32}$;
7. $1\frac{7}{8}$; **8.** $\frac{2}{3}$; **9.** 3; **10.** $5\frac{3}{4}$; **11.** $14\frac{1}{4}$;
12. $26\frac{2}{5}$; **13.** $\frac{1}{6}$; **14.** $\frac{3}{14}$; **15.** $\frac{1}{5}$; **16.** $\frac{1}{4}$;
17. $\frac{2}{9}$; **18.** $1\frac{3}{7}$; **19.** $5\frac{20}{27}$; **20.** $473\frac{11}{16}$; **21.** 42;
22. $\frac{1}{12}$

Part 4: **1.** 1; **2.** $9 \times \frac{7}{8}$; **3.** $1{,}000 \times 2\frac{2}{3}$;
4. 100×10; **5.** $82 \times 1\frac{1}{16}$; **6.** 698;
7. $4\frac{3}{4}$; **8.** $8\frac{1}{4}$

Part 5: **1.** $\frac{1}{48}$; **2.** $\frac{1}{48}$; **3.** $\frac{1}{14}$; **4.** 45; **5.** 60;
6. 54; **7.** $\frac{1}{18}$, $\frac{1}{18} \div 5 = \frac{1}{90}$; **8.** 4, $4 \div \frac{1}{9} = 36$